what

English translation by Baobab Books • Original edition published in German under the title *Etwas Schwarzes* © 2017 by Baobab Books, Basel, Switzerland • All rights reserved. Published by Orchard Books, an imprint of Scholastic Inc., *Publishers since 1920.* ORCHARD BOOKS and design are registered trademarks of Watts Publishing Group, Ltd., used under license. SCHOLASTIC and associated logos are trademarks and/or registered trademarks of Scholastic Inc. • The publisher does not have any control over and does not assume any responsibility for author or third-party websites or their content. • No part of this publication may be reproduced, stored in a retrieval system, or transmitted in any form or by any means, electronic, mechanical, photocopying, recording, or otherwise, without written permission of the publisher. For information regarding permission, write to Scholastic Inc., Attention: Permissions Department, 557 Broadway, New York, NY, 10012. • This book is a work of fiction. Names, characters, places, and incidents are either the product of the author's imagination or are used fictitiously, and any resemblance to actual persons, living or dead, business establishments, events, or locales is entirely coincidental. • LIBRARY OF CONGRESS CATALOGING-IN-PUBLICATION DATA AVAILABLE • ISBN 978-1-338-53019-3 • 10 9 8 7 6 5 4 3 2 1   20 21 22 23 24

Printed in China   38 • First edition, April 2020 • The text type was set in Tuffy Bold. • The display type was set in Block Berthold. • The illustrations were created using oil paint and crayons. • Book design by Marijka Kostiw

Could That Be?

by **REZA DALVAND**

Orchard Books　　New York

One day, the forest gleamed

in colors more beautiful

than ever before.

There in a clearing,

between trees that

glittered green and red,

lay something small.

Well, what could that be?

The leopard stopped mid-stroll. She went slowly closer to examine it. "This looks like one of my spots!" she declared. "It must have fallen off while I was hunting yesterday. I have to warn the others, before they all lose their spots!"

And away she ran.

A crow circled high in the sky, when suddenly she saw

something glint on the ground. She dove down and turned

the object over with her beak. "I bet that's a piece of a star . . .

it won't take long for the whole sky to collapse!"

Flustered, she flew away to tell the others.

The crow's caw attracted the fox. He followed the sound and saw something strange on the ground. He sniffed it thoroughly but could not work out what it was.

He thought about it some more.

The fox had heard a lot about the king's palace. "I bet that's the princess's jewel," he muttered to himself. "The wind must have rolled it here. The princess will have cried a lot over the lost jewel, so the king will send out his army to look for it. I have to warn everybody, so that they can escape the soldiers!"

And quickly he left.

The bear thought the object was a bit of

horseshoe from the hoof of a warhorse.

The enemy was near!

The owl with her great night vision

saw the glistening shape below

and was certain it was a

dragon's egg.

The dragon might hatch

soon and set the whole forest on fire!

The

cat

thought

the lump

was her

poo and

quickly

covered

it up.

By now there was complete confusion in the forest. All the animals far and wide reported what they had seen: the spot of a leopard, a piece of a star, a lost horseshoe . . . and a thousand other curiosities that you could find in the world.

Everybody was very excited about the mystery.

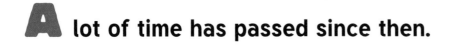 lot of time has passed since then.

In the clearing, between trees that glitter

green and red, still lies something small.

Perhaps the seed of a beautiful sapling,

or a piece of chocolate,

or a bag of coins.

But perhaps it is something that only

you know: something mysterious,

something lovely, something magical . . .

What do *you* think that could be?

31192021984651